GOOD NIGHT!
GOOD NIGHT!

CARIN BERGER

Greenwillow Books

An Imprint of HarperCollinsPublishers

For Thea, who has always been much too busy to say good night.
With special thanks to Porter Gillespie for the photography and
Dagmar Daley and Catherine Lazure for the textile expertise.

Good Night! Good Night!
Copyright © 2017 by Carin Berger
All rights reserved. Manufactured in China.
For information address HarperCollins Children's Books,
a division of HarperCollins Publishers,
195 Broadway, New York, NY 10007.
www.harpercollinschildrens.com

Collages were used to prepare the full-color art.
The text type is 28-point Perpetua.

Library of Congress Cataloging-in-Publication Data is available.
ISBN 978-0-06-240884-6 (hardcover)

17 18 19 20 21 SCP 10 9 8 7 6 5 4 3 2 1
First Edition

Greenwillow Books

Good night! *Good night!*
It's sleepy time.

Good-night stories.

Good-night songs.

Good-night hugs.

Good-night kisses.

Good-night hugs. *Again*. Good-night . . .

DANCeS!

dances?

What? Okay.
Good-night dances.

Here we go . . .

Good-night stories.

Good-night songs.

Good-night hugs.

Good-night kisses.

Good-night hugs. *Again*.

Good-night dances.

And good-night . . .

monsters?

There are **no** monsters here. Really.

There is nothing under the bed. I'll check.

Oh! Nothing *except* . . .

BUNNY!
All righty. Let's see.
Good-night stories.
Good-night songs.
Good-night hugs.
Good-night kisses.
Good-night hugs. *Again*.
Good-night dances.
Good night, Bunny.
And good night . . .

JUMPING BEANS!

jumping beans?

1

Oh, dear.

Okay. Okay. Jumping beans.

3 jumps. One. Two. Three.

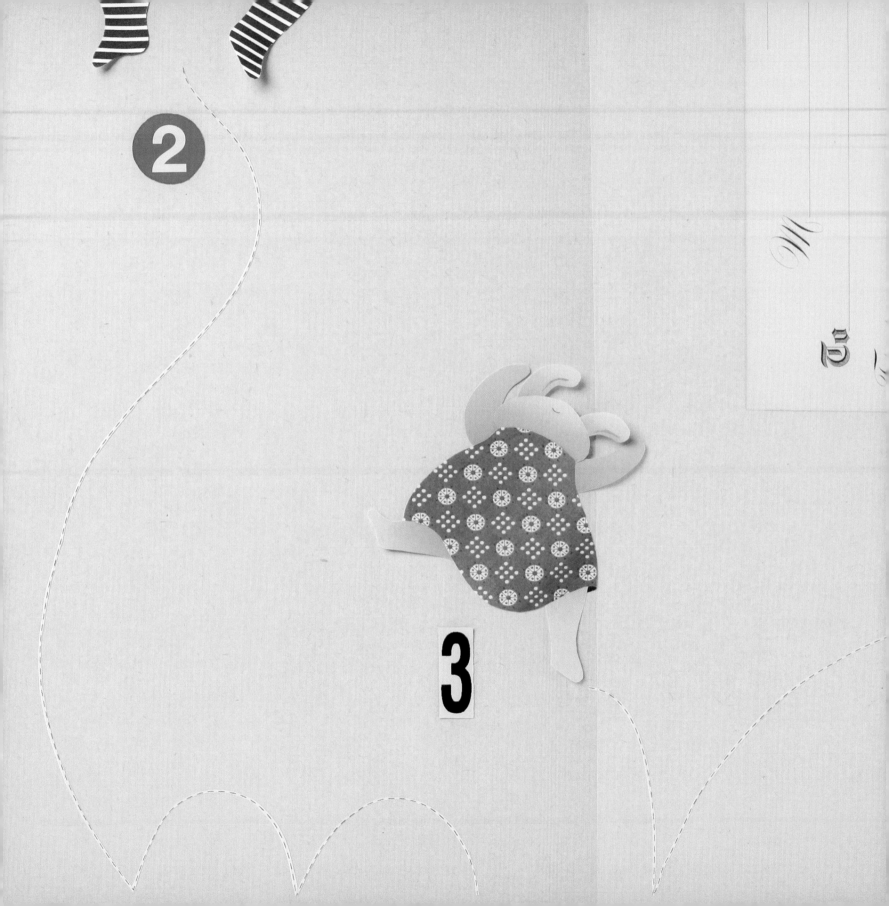

Now . . .

Good-night stories.

Good-night songs.

Good-night hugs.

Good-night kisses.

Good-night hugs. *Again.*

Good-night dances.

Good night, Bunny.

Good night, jumping beans.

Good night . . .

MONKEYS!!

monkeys?

Oh no!
Not monkeys!
Naughty monkeys.
It's bedtime.

Okay. One last time . . .

Good-night stories.

Good-night songs.

Good-night hugs.

Good-night kisses.

Good-night hugs. *Again*.

Good-night dances.

Good night, Bunny.

Good night, jumping beans.

And just one little monkey kiss.

Good-night sips.

Good-night snuggles. Good night . . .

No. No tickles.

Good-night tiptoes.

Good-night whispers.

Shhhhhhhhhhhhhh . . .

Good night, my loves . . .

Good night.

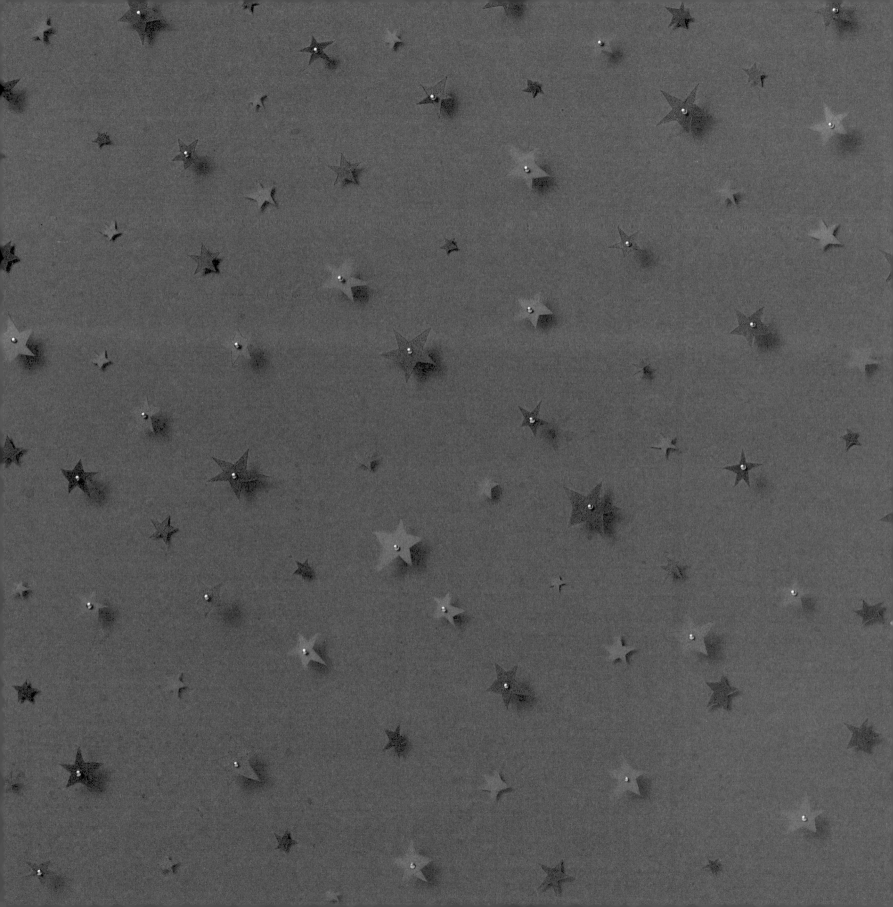